THE
THIRTEENTH
ROSE

THE THIRTEENTH ROSE

GAIL BOWEN

RAVEN BOOKS
an imprint of
ORCA BOOK PUBLISHERS

Library and Archives Canada Cataloguing in Publication

Bowen, Gail, 1942-
The thirteenth rose / Gail Bowen.
(Rapid reads)

Also issued in electronic format.
ISBN 978-1-4598-0225-4

I. Title. II. Series: Rapid reads
PS8553.O8995T55 2013   C813'.54   C2012-907309-1

First published in the United States, 2013
Library of Congress Control Number: 2012952480

Summary: It's Valentine's night, and late-night radio talk-show host
Charlie D's planned discussion of love and satisfaction is derailed when
a vigilante group promises to kill one prostitute each hour
and post their murders live online.

*Orca Book Publishers is dedicated to preserving the environment and has
printed this book on Forest Stewardship Council® certified paper.*

Orca Book Publishers gratefully acknowledges the support for
its publishing programs provided by the following agencies:
the Government of Canada through the Canada Book Fund and the
Canada Council for the Arts, and the Province of British Columbia
through the BC Arts Council and the Book Publishing Tax Credit.

Design by Teresa Bubela
Cover photography by Getty Images

ORCA BOOK PUBLISHERS   ORCA BOOK PUBLISHERS
PO Box 5626, Stn. B   PO Box 468
Victoria, BC Canada   Custer, WA USA
V8R 6S4   98240-0468

www.orcabook.com
Printed and bound in Canada.

16 15 14 13 • 4 3 2 1

For Stefani Langenegger, with love.

CHAPTER ONE

F or the hustlers in my neighborhood, the evening of February 14 is bigger than Christmas. No one wants to spend the last hours of Valentine's Day alone. And Shuter Street is the place to connect. Even the midwinter slush can't dampen the festive mood. Everybody wants to party. The hookers, in their lipstick-red, thigh-high boots, offer clients a buffet of sexual pleasures. Drug dealers offer their own buffet, an array of goodies that can perk you up or take you out—buyer's choice.

When Dolores O'Reilly calls my name from across the street, something in her voice catches my attention. Dolores has been working Shuter Street for as long as I can remember. Her days as a dewy Irish rose are long past. She's giving Father Time a run for his money. But there's more brass than copper in Dolores's shoulder-length curls. Her eyes are tired too. She's seen too much.

"Happy Valentine's Day, Charlie D," she says. There is no mistaking the sadness in her voice. I'm carrying thirteen long-stemmed scarlet roses for my producer, Nova Langenegger. I cross the street, pluck one of the roses from the florist's wrapping and hand it to Dolores.

She holds the deep-red blossom against her cheek. "You didn't have to do that, Charlie D," she says. "But I'm glad you did."

"Bad night?"

She nods. "The worst. That O'Hanlon guy you've got working at your station is trouble. He's frothing at the mouth about cleaning up the red-light district."

"Kevin O'Hanlon is a mean dog," I agree. "He's always growling and snapping at something. His ratings are through the roof. But I don't think people take him seriously."

"You're wrong, Charlie D." Dolores lights a Player's Plain and drags deeply. "Kevin O'Hanlon has a following. They call themselves O'Hanlon's Warriors, and they're making life hell for sex workers."

"Are they harassing you?"

She raises an eyebrow. "You have no idea," she says. "At first it was just name-calling. And what the cops call 'inappropriate touching.' Then O'Hanlon's Warriors got creative. They started a one-page newspaper called—are you ready?—*SLUT ALERT*. It's about what you'd expect. Pictures of girls

3

on the stroll. Obscene cartoons. Lists of the license numbers of johns. Now the word on the street is that the Warriors are beating up both girls and johns."

"If people are getting hurt, you should go to the police."

Dolores widens her eyes in disbelief. "Jeez, Charlie, were you born yesterday? In this neighborhood, cops are not our friends. Besides, we don't have proof that O'Hanlon's Warriors have hurt anybody. All we have are rumors." She takes another drag on her cigarette. "Whatever they're doing, the Warriors have really cut into business. I've been out here for two hours and not even a sniff."

I smile. "A knockout like you? That must be hard on your ego."

"Like I have any ego left after all these years." Dolores laughs, but the Player's Plains have taken their toll. Her laugh ends in a coughing fit. "My New Year's resolution is to quit smoking," she says.

"New Year's is eleven months away," I say.

She winks. "Lucky for me, huh?" Dolores takes a final puff of her cigarette. Then she throws it to the sidewalk and grinds it out with the toe of her boot. "Time to get back to work."

"Why don't you take the night off?" I say. "Go home. Pour yourself a glass of that vin rose you like and listen to Leonard Cohen."

"A girl's got to pay the rent," Dolores says. She tries a smile, but she's had a procedure to plump out her lips, and they remain frozen.

A late-model suv turns the corner. Dolores waves her rose at the driver, and he slows. Her face brightens.

"You brought me luck, Charlie," she says. "Leonard Cohen's going to have to take a cold shower."

She approaches the car, exchanges a few words with the driver and slides into the front seat. Over the years, I've seen Dolores hop into a hundred cars. I turn my attention to something that's a real novelty.

A black Rolls-Royce is purring down the street toward CVOX ("ALL TALK/ALL THE TIME"), the radio station where I do the late-night call-in show. We don't see many Rolls-Royces in our neighborhood. But I know who's inside this one.

Tonight's guest expert on *The World According to Charlie D* is Misty de Vol Burgh, the twenty-five-year-old bride of eighty-three-year-old billionaire Henry Burgh. Our Valentine's Day topic is satisfaction—specifically, how to curl your partner's toes and make him or her beg for more.

Before her marriage, Misty was a high-priced escort. She knows a thing or two about toe curling. In the past year, she's also been learning a thing or two about running a radio station. As his wedding gift to his bride, Henry Burgh bought her CVOX. Misty is now my boss. So far she is doing a bang-up job. I quicken my pace so I can welcome her.

The driver is helping Misty out of the Rolls when I arrive. Lighting Misty's way are the neon call letters on the roof of CVOX. The O in CVOX is an open mouth with red lips and a tongue that looks like Mick Jagger's. It may be tacky, but for eleven years that sign has said *Welcome home* to me.

When Misty steps onto the sidewalk, the driver holds her arm as if she were spun glass. She and Henry are expecting their first child any day now. As she smooths her coat over the swell of her pregnancy, the light from the call letters bathes Misty's face in a rosy glow. She has always been a very pretty woman. Tonight, brimming with anticipation, she is beautiful.

The streets are slick, so I take Misty's arm and lead her toward the door. Out of nowhere, the image of Dolores hopping into the suv to have sex with a man she's never met flashes through my mind. Luck is a funny thing. Some people have it. Some people don't.

Someone has taped a copy of *SLUT ALERT* on the door of the entrance to CVOX. I grab it and try to crush it into a ball before Misty sees it. She's too fast for me. She takes the paper from my hand, smooths it out and looks at the caricature. It's a cartoon of Misty and Henry. Both are naked. They're having sex on a mountain of money. The caption is chilling. "Sexually transmitted diseases kill. Kill a whore before she kills you."

Misty leans toward me. "Nice," she says drily. She looks again at the cartoon. "You know what's really sad? Whoever did this has talent. Why would someone with that kind of ability waste his time on hate?"

Without waiting for an answer, Misty takes out her cell and hits speed dial. As she speaks to her husband, her voice takes on a special tenderness. "Henry, it's me. Everything's fine. I just wanted to hear your voice." She laughs softly. "No, I don't need you to come down here. I need you to stay at home, listen to Charlie's show and keep our bed warm."

After Misty breaks the connection, we pass the security desk and make our way down the hall. The walls are hung with oversized black-and-white photos of CVOX's on-air personalities. *The World According to Charlie D* is our station's top-rated show. My photo has pride of place at the end of the hall, but Misty stops at the first picture on her right.

It's of Kevin O'Hanlon. In the photo he looks like a stand-up guy. Lots of hair, a snub nose, freckles and a boyish grin. But in person, Kevin can't hide the fact that he's a creep. There's real ugliness in the curve of his mouth, and his body is always tense with anger. On air, his voice is hectoring. He treats his callers badly—interrupting, shouting, belittling, even cutting off callers who disagree with him. His fans love him. People who disagree with his right-wing politics tune in just to see what he'll do next.

Misty stares at O'Hanlon's picture for a long time. "What do you think of him?" she says finally.

"I think he's a prick," I say.

Misty nods. "That's my opinion too, but his ratings are phenomenal." She smiles. "You're still number one, though."

"Thanks for noticing," I say. "Time for us to join Nova—the woman responsible for keeping our show at the top."

No one is more surprised at the success of *The World According to Charlie D* than Nova and me. We offer our listeners standard fare—riffs on the topic of the day, a few tunes and a chance to listen in as I chat with our callers. Most nights, we just keep our listeners company in the small hours. Once in a while we do good work. Over the years we've kept more than a few people from hurting themselves or others.

I'm aware of my limitations. I'm not a shrink or a social worker. If we have a seriously troubled caller, we always arrange for follow-up treatment with a professional. If a caller poses a real threat, we contact the authorities. As I see it, my job is to be there for our listeners—not judging, just listening. So far, my approach seems to have worked.

I glance down at Nova's scarlet roses and at the pink-and-white teddy bear I bought for her two-year-old daughter, Lily. Tonight's Valentine's show was supposed to be as sweet and frothy as a girlie drink. The copy of SLUT ALERT taped to the front door has left a bitter taste in my mouth. By inviting the public to "kill a whore before she kills you," O'Hanlon's Warriors have crossed the blood-red line that separates harmless crackpots from the dangerously disturbed. The cartoon on the door was a warning. As I shepherd Misty down the hall toward Studio D, my spidey senses are tingling. It's going to be a long night.

CHAPTER TWO

When I enter the control room, the scene is reassuringly normal. I exhale. It's possible my spidey senses are in need of a tune-up. Nova, who invented multitasking, has a phone balanced between her ear and her shoulder. She is keying into her computer. On her desk, there's a plastic container filled with heart-shaped cookies. The pink icing on the cookies is studded with cinnamon hearts. Lily's work. I'd recognize it anywhere.

Nova spots the roses and gives me a mile-wide grin. Then she disentangles herself from her phone, jumps up, hugs Misty and claims her bouquet.

"Charlie, these are gorgeous." I hand Nova the pink-and-white bear. She grimaces. "I'm such a loser. All Lily and I got you were the cookies."

"That's plenty," I say. "They're works of art."

"That's exactly what they are," Nova says. "Don't eat them. That cookie dough spent more time on the floor than in the mixing bowl."

"Nothin' says lovin' like something from the floor," I say. I pick up the container of cookies and lead Misty into the dark coolness of the studio.

"Here's the setup," I say. "There's not much to explain." I point to the glass partition that separates us from the control room. "When we're on air, Nova and I communicate through hand signals, our talkback microphones and our computers. The speakers in the control room are always on, so Nova can hear me and the show without earphones." I pass Misty her earphones. "We need to keep these on when we're on air," I say. "If Nova wants to talk to me not on air, she uses a talkback microphone. You won't hear the talkback unless you want to. Most guests find it distracting. If something comes up that we both need to hear, Nova can change the setting."

Misty listens to my explanation solemnly. I smile at her. "Relax," I say. "You're in good hands. There's a technician down the hall. I make mistakes, but Nova doesn't. We need to do a quick soundcheck. I'm going to turn on your mic, and you tell me what you had for breakfast."

Misty dimples. "Heart-shaped waffles with fresh strawberries and whipped cream."

"Tasty!" I say.

In the control room, Nova holds up five fingers. She counts down. Our theme music, "Ants Marching" by the Dave Matthews Band, begins. When the music fades, it's my turn. I lean into my microphone and dig for my radio voice—deep, reassuring and intimate.

"Good evening. I'm Charlie Dowhanuik, and you are listening to The World According to Charlie D.

"Love is in the air. It's February four-teenth—Valentine's Day. Ogden Nash celebrated the occasion with a three-line poem.

I claim there ain't

Another saint

As great as Valentine.

"If you share Mr. Nash's view, and your day was perfect in every way, raise a glass to Cupid and count your blessings. If you're sitting alone with an empty box of chocolates, half a bottle of flat champagne and the feeling

that everybody had fun at the party but you, stay tuned.

"Our theme tonight is satisfaction, which my dictionary defines as 'the act of satisfying or of being satisfied.' Joining me in studio is Misty de Vol Burgh. Misty has some intriguing thoughts about how we can satisfy our romantic partners and ourselves.

"On the old TV show M*A*S*H, Hawkeye once asked what we were worth without love. Hawkeye was a doctor. His answer was that without love, all we are is eighty-nine cents' worth of chemicals walking around lonely. A definite downer on this day of hearts and flowers. Misty believes that we can do magic with those eighty-nine cents' worth of chemicals. So kick back, listen and learn.

"Welcome, Misty. It's good to have you with us tonight."

As she leans into the microphone, Misty's soft, blond hair falls forward, brushing her cheek. Her peaches-and-cream complexion is the real thing. Her lips are deep pink, full and sensual. Henry Burgh is one lucky guy to be warming the bed he and Misty will share tonight.

"It's good to be here," she says. Her voice is rich and musical—a good voice for radio.

Misty levels her gaze at me. *"I notice that you skipped over my credentials for speaking about intimacy. I'm not ashamed of my past, Charlie. Before I fell in love with Henry, I was an escort. The amount of money I earned depended on how completely I satisfied my customers. No girl in the city earned more than I did. I'm not boasting. I just want your listeners to know that I've learned techniques that can help them."*

I glance over at the control booth. Nova is giving Misty the thumbs-up.

"Thanks for your candor, Misty," I say. *"So as someone who satisfied men professionally, what works?"*

I've watched amateurs handling microphones before. Most often, they don't trust the mic to do its job. They're constantly fiddling with it. Misty's a natural. She treats her microphone as if it's an extension of herself. As one more part of her that can reach out to another human being.

"The sexual component is always there," she says, "especially on a first date, and my customers paid eight hundred dollars an hour for a three-hour minimum."

"That's a substantial investment," I say.

She shrugs. "The equivalent of a weekend at a nice hotel in New York. Or a meal with friends at a hot new restaurant. I made certain my clients got their money's worth."

"Three hours is a long time," I say. "There must have been some spectacular feats of endurance."

Misty shakes her head. "Nothing beyond the usual. The actual sex always took a very small proportion of the time. But early in my career, I learned that the first minutes of a date and the time the client and I spent together after we'd had sex were the key to real client satisfaction."

"Any tips for our listeners?" I ask.

Misty laughs. "Nothing exotic. Just a little acting exercise. Before I went into a hotel room to be with a client, I'd close my eyes and tell myself that the man on the other side of the door was the man I loved. I hadn't seen him for weeks. And I couldn't wait to be with him."

"You made your clients feel they mattered," I say.

Misty's voice is level. "We all want to believe we matter. I made my clients feel there was nowhere I would rather be than with them. It worked. My clients always came back to me. They could have gotten sex anywhere. What they cherished was the welcome I gave them and the time we shared afterward."

"They wanted the closeness," I say. As soon as the words leave my mouth, I remember how good it felt to lie beside the woman I loved, and talk. Ariel's been dead three years.

I can still hear the sound of her laughter in the dark. My mind drifts. Luckily, Misty stays on topic.

"You're right, Charlie," she says. *"People are hungry for someone who will listen and not judge."*

I pull myself back to the present. *"That's pretty much what I do every night on the show,"* I say.

The glint in Misty's eyes is mischievous. *"Do you earn eight hundred dollars an hour with a three-hour minimum?"*

I furrow my brow. *"I'm going to need a calculator for that one,"* I say. *"But while I figure out my hourly worth, let's have a listen to Mick Jagger singing 'Satisfaction'— the anthem for those of us who can never quite manage to get it together."*

I sing the opening bars along with Mick. Nova and Misty shoot me the kind of look sisters give kid brothers who are showing off. I open up my talkback.

"Mick may be getting a little long in the tooth, but he can still nail the pain," I say. Nova rolls her eyes. She is not a fan of the Stones.

The callboard is lit up like the proverbial Christmas tree. The Inbox is already close to full. I turn to Misty. "Your dance card is filling up," I say. "Satisfaction is obviously a hot topic."

I cast a fleeting look in Nova's direction. Knowing she's there always anchors me. Nova's a truly terrific woman—smart, compassionate and real. She never wears makeup. She doesn't need to. Her skin is flawless. Her eyes are the clear blue-gray of a northern lake. When she's working, she ties her blond hair up in a scrunchy. She's thirty-four, my age, but the scrunchy always makes her look like a teenager. I watch as she takes a call. Her body tenses. Suddenly she looks like a teenager with big problems. I open the talkback.

"What's up?" I say.

She doesn't answer. Her focus is wholly on the caller. Her thumbnail finds its way into her mouth—always a bad sign. Her nails are already chewed to the quick. Finally, the call is over. When Nova opens her talkback, her voice is small and strained. "That phone call…" she says. "I hope it was a prank, but I don't think it was."

"Did you recognize the voice?" I ask.

Nova shakes her head. "No. It was a woman—at least, I think it was. The voice was muffled. But the message was clear. The caller said, 'Tell Charlie's guest to watch her step. It's take-out-the-garbage night. Time to kill all the hookers and wash the streets with blood.'"

I have no doubt that the caller is one of O'Hanlon's Warriors. I'm furious at myself. I wasn't even aware the Warriors existed until Dolores filled me in. Kevin O'Hanlon has the time slot just before mine. He sits in

the chair I sit in. He uses the microphone
I use. He's been on the air for nine months.
I had no idea he was using the microphone
we share to foment hatred.

When *The Kevin O'Hanlon Show* began,
I listened to it a few times. His attacks on
the granola-eating, Birkenstock-wearing,
holier-than-thou, left-leaning intellectuals
were nasty. But as Misty pointed out, Kevin
developed a loyal following. Over 100,000
people listened to his program every night.
Good news for CVOX. But not for the
authorities who would now have to track
down the person who had uttered the
threat. It was a needle-in-a-haystack situation. And time was running short.

Nova's voice is firm. "Charlie, we can't
handle this one alone."

I run my fingers through my hair.
"You're right," I say. "Call the police."

Misty's blue eyes are fixed on my face,
attempting to read the situation. She's nine

months pregnant. I don't want to alarm her by telling her about the phone call.

As is often the case, Nova's way ahead of me. "I'll send the police a tape of the call," she says. "And Charlie, I'll make sure they send over an officer to protect Misty."

CHAPTER THREE

I feel the first fingers of a headache pressing on the back of my skull. I reach for my aspirin and dry-swallow three. Misty watches without comment. "We may have trouble," I say, and I give her an edited version of the phone call.

Misty surprises me by not being surprised. "There've been rumors," she says. I signal Nova to change the setting on her talkback so she can hear Misty in the control room. "I still have...connections with other escorts," Misty says. "Our network pretty well covers the country. We pass along information about dangerous dates and other news that affects us professionally. Kevin O'Hanlon's Warriors have been on our radar for a while. Warriors groups have been springing up like poison mushrooms in every major city in this country."

"That's scary," I say.

"It is, and O'Hanlon's support is growing. The Warriors aren't just targeting sex workers. They're going after immigrants, Aboriginals, gays and lesbians—anyone who doesn't fit their picture of what this country should be. At the beginning, they limited their activities to hate-mongering handouts like *SLUT ALERT*."

"But they're branching out?"

Misty nods. "We've had reports of Warriors swarming their targets. There've been some serious beatings. One sex worker in this city is still in intensive care. The police strongly suspect O'Hanlon's Warriors are behind the attacks, but they don't have any proof. Until they have evidence connecting the Warriors to the attacks, their hands are tied."

"I follow the news pretty closely," I say. "Tonight's the first time I've heard about O'Hanlon's Warriors."

"They're smart enough to keep a low profile," Misty says. "The authorities haven't gone public because they don't want to cause hysteria. I don't want CVOX associated with Kevin O'Hanlon. I'd like to fire him, but our lawyers tell me firing Kevin without cause would be a publicity bonanza for him."

"So you have to keep him on the air."

Misty shrugs. "The hope is that if we give him enough rope, he'll hang himself."

"Satisfaction" ends. Mick is still unfulfilled. Nova's on the talkback. In the eleven years she's been producing our show, Nova has dealt with many crises. I've never once seen her lose her focus. Tonight is no exception.

"The officer they're sending to keep an eye on Misty will be here any minute," she says. "I'll fill him in on what we know about O'Hanlon's Warriors. Meanwhile, keep the show moving. Boomer's on line two."

Boomer is a long-time listener and an occasional caller. His rumbling bass always makes me reach for the volume control. His laugh is a bear hug.

I lean into my mic. *"Hey Boomer, it's been awhile."*

His voice warms the room. *"My lady and I listen to your show every night, Charlie D. Our routine is always the same. We ride our hogs until sundown. Then we pull into a motel and run a nice hot shower. After we've soaped each other up and toweled off, we crack open a cool one and wait until you come on the air."*

"Sounds like a good life," I say.

"It's the best," Boomer booms. *"I like what Misty said about talking. After my lady and I listen to your show, we lie side by side on*

those nice, fresh motel sheets and talk until we fall asleep. We used to worry we'd run out of things to say to each other, but we never do."

Misty's voice is playful. "So you agree that real intimacy is more than the physical act of sex."

Boomer's laugh rumbles into our headphones. Misty and I shudder and smile. "Gotta love the physical act of sex," Boomer says. "My lady and I can still give a motel mattress a workout. I'm just saying that afterward is nice, too."

"Afterward is nice," Misty says, and there's a note in her voice that catches my attention. Like everybody else, I'd assumed Misty married Henry for his money. But one look at her private smile tells me I was wrong. No matter what the cynics say, Misty de Vol Burgh is deeply in love with her husband.

On air, Boomer still has the floor.

"One more thing," he says. "Misty, my lady wanted me to thank you for not being ashamed *of your past. When her kid was little, there were times when my lady had trouble meeting the bills. She did what she had to do. Last fall, her daughter graduated as a nurse. My lady is very proud of her."* Boomer's voice is suddenly thick with emotion. *"And I'm very proud of my lady."*

"You have every reason to be proud, Boomer," Misty says. *"It was a pleasure talking to you."*

"Likewise," Boomer says. *"Happy trails, Charlie."*

"Happy trails," I say, and the heaviness that has been pressing down on my shoulders lifts.

The buoyancy doesn't last. When Nova announces our next caller, I know the good times are over.

"Lorraine's on line two," Nova says. "She's the president of Families First."

I groan. "Aren't O'Hanlon's Warriors enough grief for one night?"

"There'll be more grief if we don't put Lorraine on air," Nova says. "Families First

31

is one of the major sponsors of *The Kevin O'Hanlon Show.* They have their lawyers on speed dial."

"Kevin O'Hanlon and Families First—a marriage made in heaven," I say. I open my mic. *"Good evening, Lorraine. What's on your mind tonight?"*

"Family values," Lorraine says.

Over the years, I've learned that words can lie, but voices can't. Lorraine's voice is so sweet it makes my teeth ache. But under that sugar, there's the hiss of a snake. It doesn't take long for Lorraine to strike.

"Charlie, I simply cannot understand why you're allowing a woman like Misty de Vol on your program. I believe in hating the sin and loving the sinner. But loving the sinner doesn't mean giving a prostitute airtime to promote adultery."

My blood pressure spikes. Lorraine has just set a new world record for pushing the buttons that make me crazy. I glance over at Misty. She's unruffled. Nova looks as if she's ready to spontaneously combust. She's keying furiously into her computer. When Nova's message arrives on my computer screen, I deliver it almost verbatim to Lorraine. My bag of tricks does not include a kindly pastor voice, but I do my best.

"Lorraine, I've just been reading the mission statement of Families First. Your organization identifies itself as 'God-centered.' That leads me to a question. In a God-centered organization, shouldn't God be the one making the judgments?"

Lorraine is smooth. *"I'm sure God has already made his judgment about Misty de Vol,"* she says. I ball my fists and look longingly at the punching bag we keep in the control room for moments like this. Oblivious, Lorraine sails on. *"Our mandate at Families First is to make certain that women honor their husbands as heads of the household. A man*

33

who knows that all his physical needs will be met by his wife has no need for women like Misty de Vol."

Nova's keying into her computer again. Given the distance between me and the punching bag, I'm tempted to use the statistics Nova sends me. In the past year, Lorraine has given more than two hundred speeches to audiences throughout North America. That's a long time for a wife to absent herself from the head of the household and his physical needs. My good angel wins out. Instead of flattening Lorraine with her own record, I am courtly. *"Thank you for taking the time to call in,"* I say. *"I know how busy you are."*

The sugar in Lorraine's voice dissolves. *"I have other points to raise,"* she says.

"I'm sure you do," I say. *"But our lines are full."* Lorraine's line goes dead. In the control room, Nova raises her fingers in the peace sign.

I return her sign and check my computer screen. Next up is Olivia Newton-John singing "Physical." I introduce the tune and hum along for a few bars. Olivia's voice has an innocent, sexy bounce that almost manages to clear the air of Lorraine's poison.

I turn off my mic and lean toward Misty. "I'm very sorry about what just happened," I say. "I should have cut off Lorraine sooner."

Misty is thoughtful. "Lorraine's husband was a regular client of mine. He was the loneliest man I've ever known."

"No one would have blamed you for mentioning that on air," I say.

Misty shrugs. "I didn't want to humiliate her."

I reach over and give Misty's hand a quick squeeze. "That baby of yours is getting one terrific mother."

"Henry says he doesn't think there's a book on parenting that we haven't read," Misty says.

"It's an important job—might as well get it right," I say. We exchange a smile and sit back and listen to Olivia Newton-John. When the tune ends, I glance at my computer screen and see that Eric, a first-time caller, is on line three.

I open my mic. *"Welcome, Eric,"* I say. *"I'm glad you could join us tonight."*

"My pleasure, Charlie. I've been enjoying listening to you and Misty." Eric's voice is deep, rich and assured. He'll be good on air.

"So, Eric, what are your thoughts about getting physical?"

He laughs. *"I'm a paraplegic, so getting physical has never been a simple matter for me."*

Eric's casual reference to his paraplegia throws me. I'm not certain what tack to take, but he steers us smoothly ahead. *"Actually, my paraplegia is what prompted my call.*

Studies show that paraplegics rate regaining sexual function as more important than regaining the ability to walk."

"That's pretty solid proof that we all need intimacy," I say.

Eric chuckles. *"If you're in doubt, just ask anybody in a wheelchair. I went through adolescence wondering if I was ever going to have sex with anybody other than myself. By the time I hit high school, I'd reconciled myself to life in a wheelchair. Facing a life without intimacy was another matter. It was tough to listen to my buddies talk about the joys of sex with a partner. I was really cheesed off."*

"You don't sound cheesed off now," I say.

"I'm not," he says. *"I'm a happy man, and I owe a big part of that happiness to a sex worker named Charity. The year I graduated from high school, my buddies chipped in and bought me a night at a motel with Charity."*

"Better than a matching pen and pencil set?" I say.

"By a country mile," Eric says. *"I guess everybody's first sexual experience is daunting. If you're a paraplegic, a lot can go seriously wrong. When Charity walked into the motel room, I was scared to death. When she walked out the next morning, I'd learned how to satisfy myself and a partner."*

"Charity must have been very skilled," Misty says.

"She was," Eric says. *"And that's the reason I called in tonight. Charity was kind and patient and she knew what she was doing. She showed me that I could experience physical intimacy and that I could give pleasure to my partner. For a seventeen-year-old who believed he'd never have a normal romantic life, that was an immense gift."*

"A gift that keeps on giving," I say.

"You're right," Eric says. *"Every so often, after my wife and I make love, I think about Charity. I hope life has treated her gently."*

Misty is obviously moved, but her voice is strong. *"Thanks for telling your story, Eric.*

It meant a great deal to me. I know it meant a great deal to other sex workers. I'm glad you called in."

"So am I," Eric says.

When the call ends, Misty is in tears. She shakes her head in frustration. "Hormones," she says. It's a nice moment, but it seems all our nice moments tonight are destined to be short-lived.

Nova and I are fluent in reading one another's body language. Tonight she doesn't wait for her body to telegraph her message. Her voice comes over the talkback. "Ask Misty to announce the topic and give the call-in information," she says. "Tell her to keep talking till you're ready to go back on air."

Nova's words are a punch in the stomach. She would never hand the show over to a guest unless there was major trouble. I relay the message to Misty. Smooth as silk, she starts delivering the goods.

I exhale and open my talkback. "Okay, shoot," I say.

"There's been an email," she says tightly. "Charlie, I need you out here."

CHAPTER FOUR

*T*he *World According to Charlie D* has
been on the air eleven years. This is
the first time Nova has called me into the
control room. Her whole body is trembling.
She points to her computer screen. The
scene unfolding there is beyond horrific.
A woman is manacled to a bed. Her mouth
is stuffed with a rag to keep her from
screaming. The man is naked except for a
black cloth ski mask that covers his entire
head, exposing only his eyes. As we watch,
the man methodically plunges a knife
into the woman's body. Gouts of blood

smear the camera lens. On a night without pity, the fact that the blood clouds our vision is a small mercy.

Nova and I watch till the end. The man in the mask appears on screen. There's a clock on the wall behind him. He glances at it. "Time of the whore's death, 11:00 PM Atlantic Standard Time. The next whore will die at 11:00 Eastern Standard Time. Tune in early, Charlie D. You don't want to miss the execution. To find us on YouTube, just type in the search words *live murder whore.*"

The cop sent to guard Misty de Vol has arrived. Wordlessly, Nova calls up Google on her computer and types in YouTube and the search words. The video begins again. Nova buries her face in her hands.

"I can't," she says. The young cop watches for a few minutes and then vomits in Nova's wastebasket. Pale and shaking, he carries the wastebasket out into the hall.

When he comes back into the control room, he announces that he's called for backup.

I focus on Misty. She's using Eric's story about Charity as a jumping-off point to discuss the importance of human touch in our lives. Her voice carries the quiet authority of a person who knows what she's talking about. She's doing fine. I shoot her a grateful glance and turn back to my producer.

Nova's blue-gray eyes are wide with terror. "Charlie, they're going to kill another woman. All we know is that she'll be dead by eleven o'clock Eastern Standard Time." Nova glances up at the clock on the control-room wall. "That's twenty-five minutes from now. They must have waited before they sent the email with the link to us. The woman could be anywhere in that time zone. There's no way we can stop this."

My head feels as if it's caught in a vise. I've read the aspirin bottle. I'm familiar with the recommended daily dosage. I shake three more tablets into my palm and dry-swallow them.

"There's one possibility," I say. "O'Hanlon's Warriors addressed me by name in the email. That means they're listening to the show. If we can get Kevin to come to the studio and go on air, he'll be able to call off his goons."

"Do you think that will work?"

I shrug. "It's all we've got," I say.

Nova is fighting for control, but her voice is firm. "Misty should be the one to call Kevin O'Hanlon. She owns the station. He'll have to listen to her. We'll go to music—Marvin Gaye and 'Sexual Healing.'"

I stand to go back into the studio. My legs are leaden, but as I slide into the chair next to Misty's, my pulse slows. She's talking about how a skilled masseuse can give a sense of connection to someone who's alone. I try to remember the last time I had an intimate physical connection with anyone. I can't. Maybe I should ask Misty for the name of a good masseuse.

I give Misty the thumbs-up, reach for my Charlie D voice and open my mic. *"Here's Marvin Gaye begging his beloved to wake up and lay a little canoodling on him. Marvin doesn't hold back. Don't you hold back either. Valentine's Day is almost over. Draw your lover near. Let Marvin's heat light your fire. It's time for a little 'Sexual Healing.'"*

I turn off my mic and move closer to Misty.

"We've got trouble," I begin.

There is no way I can sugarcoat the facts. One woman has already been killed. Another woman has been marked for death. No one can know where it will end. Misty listens without comment, then picks up our landline and calls her husband.

The subject of Misty's call to Henry is grim. But when she speaks to her husband, her voice is a caress. A man could get lost in that voice. Billionaires are used to making decisions quickly. Misty's phone call to Henry Burgh lasts less than a minute. After she breaks the connection, she flips the switch that brings Nova into the conversation. She gives Nova the thumbs-up sign.

"Henry volunteered to call Kevin O'Hanlon, but this is my station. I'll deliver the message." She lowers her eyes. "Henry's on his way down to CVOX. He's very protective of me."

Misty picks up the landline, hits speed dial and puts the call on speakerphone. When she talks to Kevin, Misty doesn't sound like a woman who needs protecting.

Kevin is livid. He rants about violating what he calls "the contract of trust" between him and his audience. He shouts about a violation of his Charter rights. He hints darkly at a lawsuit against CVOX. He threatens to bring in his lawyer. Misty hears him out, then says, "You're wasting my time. If your ass isn't here in the studio within fifteen minutes, you're fired."

Kevin slams down the receiver and Misty smiles sweetly.

"He'll be here," she says.

Nova seems to have gotten her second wind.

"Okay," she says. "Let's do what we can to salvage this show. Holiday's over, Charlie D. You're back on—Katy Perry with 'Teenage Dream.'"

I flip on my mic and lean in. *Time to regroup,* I say. *"Time to remember how it felt the first time you were in love and ready to make the big move and go all the way. Here's Katy Perry with 'Teenage Dream.'"*

As soon as Katy hits the first line, Misty picks up her cell phone. "I'm going to make some calls," she says. "Some of the other girls in town might be able to name men who hate sex workers enough to be part of this scheme."

The control room is now a sea of blue. The colleagues of the young cop with the weak stomach have arrived. I listen to Katy and try to keep my eyes from watching the second hand on the clock. We are now ten minutes away from the Eastern Standard Time killing.

Katy Perry is singing about getting into her skintight jeans. I know she's just about to make her teenage dream come true. I also know that we're close to the end of the tune.

I tell myself I have to carry on as if it's business as usual. I take the next call. A retired nurse named Patsy is on the line. Her husband is in hospital, dying. Patsy remembers how important touch was to the babies she cared for during her career. Every night, she squeezes into the hospital bed with her husband. Patsy says that although her husband doesn't recognize her anymore, she believes her presence comforts him. When Patsy finishes her story, Misty's eyes well up. She blames her tears on hormones. I have no excuse for mine.

Our next caller is a young woman named Destiny who buys lingerie on the sale table and cuts away at the seams to weaken the garments. She and her beloved are into rough sex. They both get turned on when he rips her undies off.

Nova puts Madonna's "Erotica" on the playlist. It's a celebration of lovers who enjoy the twinning of pleasure and pain. As Madonna sings the first line, I can almost hear Destiny's dainties ripping. My fantasies are cut short when Nova's voice comes over the talkback.

"Kevin O'Hanlon just called in. He's stuck in traffic. He'll be delayed."

I look at the clock—eight minutes till the next killing. There's not a doubt in my mind that Kevin is stalling, showing us he won't be pushed around. If another woman dies because Kevin is flexing his muscles, I hope he rots in hell.

CHAPTER FIVE

I can't remember ever being this angry or feeling this helpless. I remind myself that our radio audience has no idea what's going on here in Studio D. All they want is someone to help them through the last hours of a day that can be painful for the loveless. It's time for business as usual. I tighten my skates and soldier on.

My computer screen shows Britney on line two. Britney is a regular. She's young and, if the photo she sent me from her high-school yearbook is any indication, very pretty. She's as self-involved as most sixteen-year-olds, but she has a sweetly crazy sense of humor. She also has a surprisingly solid understanding of why people do what they do. At this moment, Britney is exactly what our show needs.

I turn on my mic. *"Hey, it's Britney—our rainbow girl. I'm glad you called in, Brit. It's a dark night here at CVOX. We're in serious need of some color and light. So what's on your mind as the clock ticks toward the end of Valentine's Day?"*

Britney's voice is uncharacteristically solemn. *"Charlie, you and I have always had a bond. At first, it was just puppy love. But it's more than that isn't it?"*

Her confessional moment is over. Britney is ready to move along.

"Misty's right about how important it is to listen to a person you truly care about. Charlie, since your show came on the air tonight, I've been listening hard to your voice. I know something's very wrong. If you don't want to talk about it, that's okay. I just want you to know I'm

praying for you. My prayers always seem to get answered. Do you think that's weird?"

Britney's innocence is disarming. *"No, Brit. I don't think it's weird. I just hope whoever you pray to comes through for us tonight."*

"So do I," she says quietly. Then, for the first time since she began calling in, it appears Britney doesn't have anything more to say.

Silence is the enemy of talk radio, so I forge ahead.

"Brit, a lot has changed since I was in high school. What are your thoughts about what boys today want from girls and what girls today want from boys?"

Her laugh is a waterfall.

"Charlie, since the beginning of time, boys have always wanted the same thing. Girls have always had to keep them from getting what they want without hurting their feelings."

Nova opens her talkback. For a beat, she sounds like her old self.

"Give Britney a chance to bring it home, Charlie. If she's figured out a way to keep a boy's hands from wandering without hurting his feelings, the Big Gulps are on me."

I growl into my mic.

"My producer says that if you've figured out how not to give boys what they want without hurting their feelings, the Big Gulps are on her."

Brit moves in smoothly.

"It's not brain surgery. The first time a boy tried to touch something I didn't want touched, I was surprised. Then I took his hand, kissed it and moved it well away from where it shouldn't have been. The boy was the quarterback on our high-school football team—big shocker, huh?

"Anyway, he'd taken me out for a burger and a movie, and when he wasn't groping, all he could talk about was this quarterback sneak that hadn't worked out for him. So after I put a little distance between us, I asked my date what a quarterback sneak was. Then I asked why it hadn't worked out for him."

Britney inhales enough breath to get her through part two of her story.

"What happened next was totally awesome. My date suddenly looked at me as if I was a real person. When he was groping me, he was saying all this stuff about how much he cared for me and how much he'd suffer if we didn't do it. Or at least do something close to it—you know, just blue-balls talk.

Misty raises both eyebrows. I gasp. *"Brit, I don't think you meant to say that…"*

Britney's genuinely surprised. *"Blue balls is just a term kids use—it means…"*

"I know what it means, Brit," I say quickly. *"Anyway, you were saying that when you asked him about football, your date starting talking to you differently."*

"As if I was a person, instead of just a body. Football isn't exactly a passion of mine. What he said was pretty interesting though. I told him so, and just like that, his hands stopped wandering.

"Anyway, now I make it a point to find out what a boy is really interested in before we get into a wrestling match, and it always works." She pauses. "Misty, did you ever find that talking was important to your...um...clients?"

"All the time," Misty says. "Of course, my clients had paid for the sex, so that was part of the deal. But after they became regulars, I knew they looked forward to the talk afterward.

"And you're right, Britney. When my clients started to open up to me about their lives, I stopped being just a body to them and became a person. They changed too. They stopped being just bodies with physical needs and became people who were just as hopeful and as scared as we all are."

Beyond the fact that she was once an escort, I know nothing about Misty's personal history. My guess is that her path wasn't nearly as smooth and loving as Britney's. As I listen to Misty and Britney talk about how good it can be when men and women recognize one another as fellow travelers on the bumpy road to love, I realize again why I love radio. There are no false faces on radio. We're voices alone in the dark. Pretty much the way it is in real life.

It's been a hell of a night, and it's far from over, but I'm grateful for the reminder that our show can make a difference. When Nova gives me the signal that it's time to cut Misty and Britney's conversation short, I feel a pang. I open my mic.

"Time to move along," I say. *"Britney and Misty, thanks for letting us discover what girls talk about at slumber parties."*

Britney's laugh cascades.

"Oh, Charlie, if you could hear some of the things we really talk about at slumber parties, you'd be shocked. Wouldn't he, Misty?"

Misty winks at me.

"Maybe some night Brit and I should host an all-girls show," she says.

"I would absolutely loooooooove that," Britney says.

When she breaks the connection, I feel bereft.

"Let's go to music again," Nova says. "It's six minutes to twelve. We need to figure out where we go from here if that asshole Kevin doesn't show up."

My head snaps back. Nova's use of profanity is rare. But she's right. Kevin O'Hanlon may decide that the death of another human being is a small price to pay for hanging on to his role of guru to the Warriors.

I check my computer screen for the music selection and open my mic.

"Okay. On this day of men and women trying to please one another, let's check out another perspective on that age-old question. What do women want? The R&B slash reggae singer Rihanna certainly seems to have some answers. At twenty-three, she's already sold

*twenty million albums and sixty million singles.
Here she is with 'Rude Boy.'"*

Nova has the outside phone cradled between her ear and her shoulder. She's positioned herself in front of the talkback so she can relay information as it comes in. I tell Misty to put on her headphones.

Emotion always goes straight to Nova's face. A glance tells me exactly what she's feeling. Now, before Nova says a word, I know the worst has happened. Another woman is being murdered. Nova calls up the website, then turns away from her screen. "It's happening again," she says. She seems to crumple.

Then she takes a deep breath and plunges on. "The video has gone viral," she says. "A client of the woman who's being... assaulted called the police. The woman's name is Luanne Bauer. The Warrior who's doing Kevin O'Hanlon's dirty work must be a few bricks short of a load. He went to the hotel

Luanne customarily works out of. Her client recognized the room and called the cops. The Toronto cops are on their way." Nova looks at the screen and closes her eyes against the horror. "I hope to God they're in time.

"The cops here have picked up the baton. They're going to find Kevin and bring him to the studio."

I call up the website in time to see a naked man in a head mask repeatedly plunge a knife into Luanne Bauer. "Too late," I say.

I am filled with sickening rage.

The images on the screen seem to crush Misty. She folds her arms on the desk and, like a child during a grade-school rest period, places her forehead on them. I click off the website. I want to keep an eye on Misty.

"We're staying with music," Nova says. "Bruce Cockburn singing 'Lovers in a Dangerous Time.' Don't bother with an intro. But Charlie, when we come out of this song, you're going to have go on air and tell our audience what's happening."

Misty sits up, takes the pad of paper on the desk between us and begins to write. "This is Kevin O'Hanlon's resignation speech," she says. "I want to make certain he says everything he needs to say."

"Good," I say. Misty goes back to her writing. I try to collect my thoughts. My mind is blank. I have no idea what I'm going to do when "Lovers in a Dangerous Time" fades, and I have to flip on my mic and explain the unexplainable.

CHAPTER SIX

The song ends. It's my turn now.

"We're back," I say. *"And it's time for a little honesty. Britney was right when she sensed there was something wrong in* The World According to Charlie D. *We've been dealing with a nightmare here. Two very sick men in different parts of our country have killed two defenseless women. The murderers chose a method of death that robbed their victims of dignity. These men believe they're part of a mission to 'clean up' our country. For them, that means destroying everyone who isn't like them.*

"At this point, there's a great deal we don't know. Because of possible legal problems, we can't make public what we do know."

Images of the women being cut open like animals flood my mind. Suddenly, I can't speak. "Hang on, Charlie D," Nova says. "All you have to say is that this is a time for reflection, and introduce the music. It's one of the pieces that was played at Princess Diana's funeral. Sir John Tavener's 'Song for Athene.'"

I clear my throat and lean into my mic.

"I've been pondering a line from 'Lovers in a Dangerous Time'—'Never a breath you can afford to waste.' Think about that as we listen to Sir John Tavener's 'Song for Athene.' The piece was written for a woman who died too young. It was also played at the funeral of a princess. Like the women who died tonight, the princess died before her time."

From the moment the Westminster Abbey Choir starts to sing the first lines—*Alleluia. / May flights of angels sing thee to thy rest*—there is silence in the control room and in the studio. We are hungry for comfort. And, for four minutes, we find solace in the beauty of Tavener's music. When the choir sings the final lines— *Alleluia. / Weeping at the grave creates the song: Alleluia. / Come, enjoy rewards and crowns I have prepared for you*—the young cop with the queasy stomach is crying openly. He is not alone.

I open my mic and ask for a moment of silence. At that point the cops bring in Kevin O'Hanlon. All hell breaks loose.

Kevin is not honored to have a police escort. In fact, he is livid. Kevin is a banty rooster of a guy. He's short. So were Winston Churchill, Ghandi and Martin Luther King. Each of them found a way to make his mark without spewing hate.

It appears Kevin has decided that strutting and making a lot of noise will buy him a ticket to immortality. He's red-haired, and tonight his pale skin is flushed with fury. Kevin cannot tolerate opposition. Tonight he can't stop yelling. He yells at the cops. He yells at me. He yells at Nova. We're just pawns in the game. Kevin is the king. When he steps into the studio, he makes a fatal mistake. He treats Misty as yet another pawn.

Henry Burgh enters the control room just in time to witness the face-off between Kevin and Misty. Misty hands Kevin the handwritten letter of resignation she's been working on.

"Read this on air, word for word," she says, and her voice is steel. "No additions. No deletions. Just read what's written on this page."

Kevin skims the words.

"I'm not going to read this shit. I'm not going to crawl." His eyes turn to Misty. "I'm certainly not going to crawl for a slut."

Henry is in time to hear Kevin's ugly words. He may be eighty-three years old, but Henry Burgh has been a boxer since high school. He knows the value of the quick move.

He approaches Kevin O'Hanlon, plants his right foot slightly behind him and shifts his left foot onto the toe. Then Henry turns his body slightly and delivers a left hook that strikes Kevin squarely on the chin and knocks him out cold.

Henry steps over Kevin and embraces his wife. "Are you all right, sweetheart?"

Misty moves closer to her husband. "I'm fine, Henry."

Two cops come in and carry Kevin O'Hanlon out. He's coming to, and he doesn't look happy.

Henry kisses the top of his wife's hair, then turns to me. "What the hell is going on here?"

I give him the abbreviated version. Henry doesn't miss a beat. He reads the resignation letter Misty is holding and looks down at her fondly. "Do you want to read it on air, or shall I?"

"I'll do it," Misty says. Her voice is steady. She turns on her microphone. Her message is brief but to the point. *"Effective immediately, Kevin O'Hanlon is no longer an employee of CVOX. This station welcomes diverse opinions, but we do not give voice to hate. Tonight we witnessed the slaughter of two women by men consumed by hate. Martin Luther King Jr. said, 'Darkness cannot drive out darkness; only light can do that.' Tonight, CVOX commits itself to driving out the darkness of ignorance, bigotry and prejudice. Together, the staff of CVOX and you, our listeners and contributors, can work to defeat hate."*

Nova gives Misty a thumbs-up, but her smile is thin. The tensions of the evening have drained her. "Okay, wrap it up, Charlie. Our listeners are fragile. Give them something to hang on to that will get them through the night."

"I'm not sure I'm going to get through the night," I say. Misty and Henry, in a show of solidarity, stand behind my chair. Misty's hand is on my shoulder.

"Go to music," Nova says. "Leonard Cohen singing 'Suzanne.'"

I smile to myself. Dolores's passion for Leonard Cohen is as fervent as a teenager's. "Suzanne" is Dolores's favorite Cohen song. Nova makes up our playlists days before the show. No one could have foreseen the horror show that played itself out tonight. Dolores's date will be over by now. It makes me feel good to think of her safe at home listening to Leonard and drinking the pink wine she always refers to as "vin rosey."

I find my Charlie D voice, and when I speak into my mic, I sound like a guy who can make sense of our crazy world.

"Okay, time for a recap," I say. *"This has been one of the worst nights in the history of the show. But they say it's always darkest before the dawn. And they might just be right. Misty's words were a glimmer of light. This can be a beginning for us."*

I glance into the control room.

Another cop has just walked in. Her face is pink with cold, and there's snow on her jacket. She says something to Nova. Whatever she said is devastating. Nova buries her face in her hands. When she begins to sob, my heart sinks. I have a feeling that tonight the darkness will never end.

CHAPTER SEVEN

I hit talkback. "What's happened?"

Nova's voice is anguished. "Dolores O'Reilly was murdered tonight. The police had an anonymous tip to go to the old Waverly Hotel. That's where they found her. Same scenario as the other deaths. Dolores was manacled and raped. Then she was stabbed many, many, many times."

The marrow in my bones freezes. "How did the police know to get in touch with us?"

"Dolores's wallet had a list of people to notify in case, in her words, she 'met with tragedy,'" Nova says. Then she pounds her fist rhythmically against the desk. "Shit," she says. "Shit. Shit. Shit."

I close my eyes and see Dolores holding the rose against her cheek.

I feel like I've taken a body blow. Nova sees my reaction and goes immediately to music. It's another Leonard Cohen—"Dance Me to the End of Love."

As Leonard Cohen sings about dancing with his lover to a burning violin, I look again at Henry and Misty, and I think about luck. Who decides? Who decides that Misty and Henry will find happiness together— a happiness that, against all the odds, will end in the birth of a child who will fill their lives with joy?

Who decides that on a cold Valentine's evening, I will hand Dolores a rose that she will wave at a passing suv, and the man who is driving will slow to pick her up? Who decides that Dolores will then thank me for bringing her luck and then go to the hotel room where she will meet her death?

No matter what, I've always been able to slip into the skin of Charlie D, reach for that cool, confident voice and get through the two hours we're on the air. Tonight the show is almost over. My only job now is to do what Nova calls "the take-away"— the brief segment where I tie up the loose ends and riff about what we've learned that night.

But I can't do it. I can't find the words. I can't find my Charlie D voice. After ten seconds of dead air, the broadcast will automatically kick into a preprogrammed Muzak-type sound. That will be our sign-off. If I let that happen, I can just walk away. But somehow I can't do that either.

Dolores deserves one last Valentine.

Leonard Cohen sings the final haunting line of "Dance Me to the End of Love," and I open my mic.

"It's been a helluva night," I say, and the voice I hear is my own—unsure and frightened. *"Tonight a woman named Dolores O'Reilly was murdered. Dolores was not dealt a great hand in this life, but she played the cards she'd been given with style and courage.*

"She was a sex worker, and her workplace was the neighborhood around CVOX Radio. It's a rough area, and every night Dolores saw the worst of human nature. She never became bitter or cynical. She never let the darkness destroy her.

"She was a good friend to many in our neighborhood. If someone was sick or troubled or broke, Dolores was the first to offer help. When a john beat one of the other girls so badly that she couldn't work for weeks, Dolores took her in and cared for her. Last year, when I had what turned out to be something called walking pneumonia, Dolores brought me chicken soup every night until she decided that I'd recovered.

"Everybody has bad times. In the eleven years I've been doing The World According

to Charlie D, *I've had my share. The worst was when I lost the woman I loved. The night I found out that Ariel died, I walked out of the studio, and it was a long time before I came back. Grief did not make me a better person. I drank. I got into fights. I lashed out at everybody who tried to help. A lot of people gave up on me. Dolores never did. She never gave up on anybody. And she never gave up on life.*

"*There's a line in 'Dance Me to the End of Love' that makes my heart skip a beat. It comes when the lover asks his beloved to take him to a place where he will be 'gathered safely in.' I don't know where that place is. I just hope that tonight Dolores O'Reilly has found it.*"

I hang on until the red light signaling that my microphone is live goes to black. I can leave now.

A cop in the control room tells us that Kevin O'Hanlon has been taken to an ER. The cop says O'Hanlon was really mouthing off. He was threatening everybody. The cop is sure O'Hanlon will be all right.

Two police officers lead us down the hall. Misty and Henry walk directly behind the cops, and Nova and I follow along. Nova's winter headgear is an orange knitted cap with earflaps. She's carrying her roses and Lily's teddy bear. I'm wearing my toque and carrying the plastic container that holds Lily's heart-shaped cookies. We look like members of a bizarre religious group.

We step through the front doors into snow. The snow is falling gently in the fat, theatrical flakes that land on the hair of lovers in date movies. Henry and Misty's shining Rolls-Royce is pulled up to the curb at front. The driver is standing by the passenger door, at the ready. Henry and Misty greet him.

When Misty and Henry walk to their car, Nova and I walk with them. Henry offers to have their driver take us wherever we want to go. I look at Nova. She's a trouper, but even troupers have their limits, and Nova has reached hers.

I touch her cheek. "You go ahead," I say. "How many chances are you going to get to ride in a Rolls-Royce?"

Henry's voice is gruff. "As many as she wants," he says. "Misty and I are very grateful to you both."

"You were both pretty amazing too," I say. I turn to Nova again. "Time for you to go home," I say. "Tuck Lily's new bear in with her so she can wake up to a surprise. I'm going to hang around here for a while."

Nova and I know each other well. Her eyes meet mine. "You're going over to Dolores's corner, aren't you?"

I look down the street. The place where Dolores solicited customers is a prime location—a busy intersection with plenty of traffic. It won't be long before another girl takes it over.

Dolores liked the corner because it had a streetlight. *Enough light to give customers a glimpse*, she said, *but not so much that they can see the sags and wrinkles.*

"I'd like to pay my respects," I say.

"I'd like to pay my respects too," Nova says. She turns to Misty and Henry. "Be sure to let us know when the baby is born. I never asked. Do you know if it's a girl or a boy?"

"It's a girl," Henry says. "We're going to name her Grace, after my mother. Our daughter will be Grace de Vol Burgh."

I repeat the name. "Grace de Vol Burgh. That's a strong name, and a beautiful one." My eyes travel between Henry and his twenty-five-year-old wife. Their love for one another stings my eyes. "Grace will have a good life," I say.

Misty embraces Nova and me. Henry shakes our hands. They get into the Rolls. Nova and I watch as the shining car disappears into the snow. Then we turn and walk down to Dolores's corner.

Nova places her roses on the place where Dolores stood when she was drumming up business. She looks down at the teddy bear in her arms. "I wonder if anyone ever gave Dolores a teddy bear," she says.

"Don't go there," I say. And then I kneel in the snow and say the prayer that my mother and I said together every night until the night when I told her I no longer believed in God. Nova kneels beside me, and together we watch the snow fall on the red petals of the roses. Only when the roses are buried do Nova and I stand up and begin the long walk home.

CHAPTER EIGHT

I t was June when Dolores O'Reilly's murderer was finally arrested. The first scorching heat had come. The hookers were wearing short skirts, midriff-baring tops and strappy stilettos. The drug dealers were sporting mirrored sunglasses and wife-beater shirts that showcased the tattoos on their thin, pale arms. Summer in the city.

Henry and Misty Burgh came down to CVOX to break the news. It was half an hour before *The World According to Charlie D* went to air. Late for a baby to be up and about, but Grace de Vol Burgh was never far from her parents' adoring eyes. Grace was a beauty. As Henry said, when it came to looks, his daughter had the good sense to choose her mother's genes.

That night, was when the Burgh family arrived, Grace was sleeping in her baby carrier. The control room was brightly lit, so we walked through to the dark quiet of the studio. As Henry gave us the account of what had happened, he kept his voice low. We all drew close to him.

It turned out that Dolores had been wrong about one thing. The police in our neighborhood *were* her friends. In fact, police all across the country had mounted an extensive undercover operation to learn the identity of the men who had killed Dolores and the other two women on the night of February 14.

The operation had been lengthy and expensive. The undercover agents approached men whom they suspected had ties to O'Hanlon's Warriors. It took months, but finally an undercover agent in our city gained the confidence of a man named Joey Shuba.

Joey was not smart, but he was powerfully built. He had two fatal flaws. He was a braggart and a heavy drinker. When Joey was drinking, he boasted about his exploits. One night he bragged to the wrong man. As soon as Joey began telling his tale of how he had killed a whore at the old Waverly Hotel, the undercover agent reached for his smartphone.

It was the beginning of the end for Kevin O'Hanlon. Joey didn't know much, but he knew just enough to lead the police to the guy who had recruited him for O'Hanlon's Warriors. After that, the police simply followed the daisy chain. Each Warrior's only connections were to the man who had recruited him and his own recruit.

It was painstaking work, but the police finally found Kevin O'Hanlon's first recruit. In return for certain considerations, the recruit was all too willing to blow the whistle on Kevin.

When Henry Burgh finishes, he sits back in his chair. "I realize that there's nothing to celebrate here," he says. "But this has been an ugly chapter in many lives. I'm glad it's finally closed."

Misty reaches for her husband's hand. "So am I," she says. "It's been a difficult time for all of us."

Hearing her mother's voice, Grace de Vol Burgh opens her eyes. When she sees me instead of her mother, she hollers. Misty picks up her daughter and murmurs reassurances. When Grace is calmed, Misty turns to me. "You two need a chance to get acquainted," she says. "Why don't you feed Grace, Charlie?"

"I'd love to," I say, "but aren't you feeding Grace the old-fashioned way?"

"I was," Misty says, "but I had to stop." Misty's blue eyes travel between Nova and me. "We haven't told anybody yet, but Henry and I decided we didn't want Grace to be an only child. We're expecting another baby in February."

I clap Henry on the back. "Way to go, Dad," I say. When I see Nova's frown, I pat Misty on the back too. "I guess you had something to do with this," I say. "Way to go, Misty."

Nova and I walk the Burgh family to the CVOX entrance. The place where Kevin O'Hanlon's picture once hung is empty. Misty is trying out a number of guest hosts. A pleasant young woman whose parents emigrated from China shortly before she was born has the inside track. Julia Wong is smart and gentle. She's also a lesbian who's especially good with young people questioning their gender identity. Nova and I are both rooting for her.

We stand in the doorway till the Burghs' Rolls-Royce turns the corner. Nova and I are not usually physically demonstrative with one another, but as we walk back down the hall, I drape my arm around her shoulder. "What do you think of Henry and Misty's news?" I say.

Nova grins. "I think it's terrific," she says. "I wish it were me. Lily's almost three. Seeing Grace has given me a bad case of baby lust."

I squeeze her shoulder. "I know what you mean. When I was feeding that little girl, I felt really happy for the first time in a long time."

Nova stops dead and gives me her no-bullshit gaze. "Is this something you and I should have a serious talk about?"

"It is," I say. "But the discussion's going to have to wait. Right now we have a show to do."

"We're not getting any younger," Nova says. "After the show let's go to Chubby's. We can drink milkshakes, eat onion rings and decide on our next move."

I kiss the top of Nova's head. "I think we've already decided on our next move," I say. "But I'm always up for Chubby's onion rings."

RAPID READS

The following is an excerpt from
Love You To Death, another exciting
Rapid Reads novel by Gail Bowen.

978-1-55469-262-0 $9.95 pb

Someone is killing some of Charlie D's
favorite listeners.

Charlie D is the host of a successful late-night radio
call-in show that offers supportive advice to troubled
listeners. *Love You to Death* takes place during one
installment of *The World According to Charlie D*—
two hours during which Charlie must discover who
is killing some of the most vulnerable members of
his audience.

CHAPTER ONE

A wise man once said 90 percent of life is just showing up. An hour before midnight, five nights a week, fifty weeks a year, I show up at CVOX radio. Our studios are in a concrete-and-glass box in a strip mall. The box to the left of us sells discount wedding dresses. The box to the right of us rents XXX movies. The box where I work sells talk radio—"ALL TALK/ALL THE TIME." Our call letters are on the roof. The O in CVOX is an open, red-lipped mouth with a tongue that looks like Mick Jagger's.

After I walk under Mick Jagger's tongue, I pass through security, make my way down the hall and slide into a darkened booth. I slip on my headphones and adjust the microphone. I spend the next two hours trying to convince callers that life is worth living. I'm good at my job—so good that sometimes I even convince myself.

My name is Charlie Dowhanuik. But on air, where we can all be who we want to be, I'm known as Charlie D. I was born with my mother's sleepy hazel eyes and clever tongue, my father's easy charm, and a wine-colored birthmark that covers half my face. In a moment of intimacy, the only woman I've ever loved, now, alas, dead, touched my cheek and said, "You look as if you've been dipped in blood."

One of the very few people who don't flinch when they look at my face is Nova ("Proud to Be Swiss") Langenegger.

For nine years, Nova has been the producer of my show, "The World According to Charlie D." She says that when she looks at me she doesn't see my birthmark—all she sees is the major pain in her ass.

Tonight when I walk into the studio, she narrows her eyes at me and taps her watch. It's a humid night and her blond hair is frizzy. She has a zit on the tip of her nose. She's wearing a black maternity T-shirt that says *Believe It or Not, I Used to Be Hot.*

"Don't sell yourself short, Mama Nova," I say. "You're still hot. Those hormones that have been sluicing through your body for nine months give you a very sexy glow."

"That's not a sexy glow," she says. "That's my blood pressure spiking. We're on the air in six minutes. I've been calling and texting you for two hours. Where were you?"

I open my knapsack and hand her a paper bag that glistens with grease from the onion rings inside. "There was a lineup at Fat Boy's," I say.

Nova shakes her head. "You always know what I want." She slips her hand into the bag, extracts an onion ring and takes a bite. Usually this first taste gives her a kid's pleasure, but tonight she chews on it dutifully. It might as well be broccoli. "Charlie, we need to talk," she says. "About Ian Blaise."

"He calls in all the time," I say. "He's doing fine. Seeing a shrink. Back to work part-time. Considering that it's only been six months since his wife and daughters were killed in that car accident, his recovery is a miracle."

Nova has lovely eyes. They're as blue as a northern sky. When she laughs, the skin around them crinkles. It isn't crinkling now. "Ian jumped from the roof of his apartment building Saturday," she says. "He's dead."

I feel as if I've been kicked in the stomach. "He called me at home last week. We talked for over an hour."

Nova frowns. "We've been over this a hundred times. You shouldn't give out your home number. It's dangerous."

"Not as dangerous as being without a person you can call in the small hours," I say tightly. "That's when the ghoulies and ghosties and long-leggedy beasties can drive you over the edge. I remember the feeling well."

"The situation may be more sinister than that, Charlie," Nova says. "This morning someone sent us Ian's obituary. This index card was clipped to it."

Nova hands me the card. It's the kind school kids use when they have to make a speech in class. The message is neatly printed, and I read it aloud. "'Ian Blaise wasn't worth your time, Charlie. None of them are. They're cutting off your oxygen.

I'm going to save you.'" I turn to Nova. "What the hell is this?"

"Well, for starters, it's the third in a series. Last week someone sent us Marcie Zhang's obituary."

"The girl in grade nine who was being bullied," I say. "You didn't tell me she was dead."

"There's a lot I don't tell you," Nova says. She sounds tired. "Anyway, there was a file card attached to the obituary. The message was the same as this one—minus the part about saving you. That's new."

"I don't get it," I say. "Marcie Zhang called in a couple of weeks ago. Remember? She was in great shape. She'd aced her exams. And she had an interview for a job as a junior counselor at a summer camp."

"I remember. I also remember that the last time James Washington called in, he said that he was getting a lot of support from other gay athletes who'd been outed, and he wished he'd gone public sooner."

"James is dead too?"

Nova raises an eyebrow. "Lucky you never read the papers, huh? James died as a result of a hit-and-run a couple of weeks ago. We got the newspaper clipping with the index card attached. Same message—word for word—as the one with Marcie's obituary."

"And you never told me?"

"I didn't connect the dots, Charlie. A fourteen-year-old girl who, until very recently has been deeply disturbed, commits suicide. A professional athlete is killed in a tragic accident. Do you have any idea how much mail we get? How many calls I handle a week? Maybe I wasn't as sharp as I should have been, because I'm preoccupied with this baby. But this morning after I got Ian's obituary—with the extended-play version of the note—I called the police."

I snap. "You called the cops? Nova, you and I have always been on the same side of that particular issue. The police operate in a black-and-white world. Right/ wrong. Guilty/innocent. Sane/Not so much. We've always agreed that life is more complex for our listeners. They tell us things they can't tell anybody else. They have to trust us."

Nova moves so close that her belly is touching mine. Her voice is low and grave. "Charlie, this isn't about a lonely guy who wants you to tell him it's okay to have a cyberskin love doll as his fantasy date. There's a murderer out there. A real murderer—not one of your Goth death groupies. We can't handle this on our own."

I reach over and rub her neck. "Okay, Mama Nova, you win. But over a hundred thousand people listen to our show every night. Where do we start?"

Nova gives my hand a pat and removes it from her neck. "With you, Charlie," she says. "The police want to use our show to flush out the killer."

 **RAPID READS**

The following is an excerpt from
One Fine Day You're Gonna Die, another
exciting Rapid Reads novel by Gail Bowen.

978-1-55469-337-5 $9.95 pb

It will take all of Charlie D's skills to
keep this Halloween from being another
"Day of the Dead."

Charlie D is back doing his late-night radio call-in
show. It's Halloween—The Day of the Dead.
His studio guest this evening is Dr. Robin Harris,
an arrogant and ambitious "expert in the arts of dying
and grieving." Charlie and Dr. Harris do not hit it
off. Things go from bad to worse when the doctor's
ex-lover goes on air to announce that he's about to
end his life.

CHAPTER ONE

Tonight as I was riding my bike to the radio station where I do the late-night call-in show, a hearse ran a light and plowed into me. I swerved. The vehicle clipped my back wheel, and I flew through the air to safety. My Schwinn was not so lucky. The hearse skidded to a stop. The driver jumped out, sprinted over and knelt beside me on the wet pavement. "Are you all right?" he asked.

I checked my essentials.

"As all right as I'll ever be," I said.

The man bent closer. The streetlight illuminated both our faces. He looked like the actor who played Hawkeye on the old TV show *M*A*S*H*. His brow furrowed with concern when he saw my cheek.

"You're bleeding," he said.

"It's a birthmark," I said.

As birthmarks go, mine is a standout. It covers half my face, like a blood mask. Nine out of ten strangers turn away when they see it. This man moved in closer.

"The doctors weren't able to do anything?" he asked.

"Nope."

"But you've learned to live with it."

"Most of the time," I said.

"That's all any of us can do," the man said, and he grinned. His smile was like Hawkeye's—open and reassuring. He offered his hand and pulled me to my feet. "I'll take you wherever you want to go," he said.

He picked up my twisted Schwinn and stowed it in the back of the hearse. I slid into the passenger seat. The air inside was cool, flower-scented and oddly soothing. After we'd buckled our seat belts, the man turned the keys in the ignition.

"Where to?" he asked.

"CVOX Radio," I said. "728 Shuter."

"It's in a strip mall," he said. "Between a store that sells discount wedding dresses and a place that rents x-rated movies."

"I'm impressed," I said. "This is a big city."

"It is," he agreed. "But my business involves pick up and delivery. I need to know where people are."

Perhaps because the night was foggy and he'd already had one accident, the driver didn't talk as he threaded his way through the busy downtown streets. When we turned on to Shuter, I saw the neon call letters on the roof of our building. The O in CVOX ("ALL TALK/ALL THE TIME") is an open mouth with red lips and a tongue that looks like Mick Jagger's. Fog had fuzzed the brilliant scarlet neon of Mick's tongue to a soft pink. It looked like the kiss a woman leaves on a tissue when she blots her lipstick.

"I'll pick you up when your show's over," the man said.

"I'll take a cab," I said. "But thanks for the offer."

He shrugged and handed me a business card. "Call me if you change your mind. Otherwise, I'll courier a cheque to you tomorrow to pay for your bike."

"You don't know my name."

The man flashed me his Hawkeye smile. "Sure I do. Your name is Charlie Dowhanuik and you're the host of 'The World According to Charlie D.' I'm a fan. I even phoned in once. It was the night you walked off the show and disappeared for a year. You were in rough shape."

"That's why I left."

"I was relieved that you did," he said. "I sensed that if you didn't turn things around, you and I were destined to meet professionally. My profession, not yours. You were too young to need my services, so I called in to remind you of what Woody Allen said."

"I remember. 'Life is full of misery, loneliness and suffering and it's over much too soon.'" I met the man's eyes. "Wise words," I said. "I still ponder them."

"So you haven't stopped grieving for the woman you lost?"

"Nope."

"But you decided to keep on living," he said.

"For the time being," I said. We shook hands, and I opened the car door and climbed out. As I watched the hearse disappear into the fog, the opening lines of an old schoolyard rhyme floated to the top of my consciousness.

Do you ever think when a hearse goes by
That one fine day you're gonna die?
They'll wrap you up in a cotton sheet
And throw you down about forty feet.
The worms crawl in,
The worms crawl out...

There was more, but I had to cut short my reverie. It was October 31. Halloween. The Day of the Dead. And I had a show to do.